ICONS AS RESISTANCE

CHALLENGING THE NEW ICONOCLASM IN THE CATHOLIC CHURCH

Marcelle Bartolo-Abela

First published in 2017 by
HOPE AND LIFE PRESS

The cover shows a photograph of an icon of Mandylion of Edessa written by a grandmother in Ukraine.

Published by
HOPE AND LIFE PRESS
2312 Chemin Herron #A, Dorval QC, H9S 1C5 Canada; and
P.O. Box 37, East Longmeadow, MA 01028, USA.

Printed in the United States of America.

INTRODUCTION

This book is the result of a series of conversations held earlier this year at *St. Corbinian's Bear,* the virtual home of former criminal defense attorney and award-winning Catholic author Timothy Capps.

ICONS, THE CHURCH AND THE PEOPLE OF GOD

A thick piece of wood. Clay. Chalk, linen and the skin of rabbits. Colored dirt from various regions of the earth. Duck eggs, vinegar and water. Gold or silver. The very breath of the human person and an agate stone. Fur from the tail of martens or squirrels. Oil of the flax plant.

That is an icon. Or is it?

Icons and the Church

While in the period of iconoclasm, the Church struggled for the icon, in our time it is the icon that struggles for the Church (Leonid Ouspensky).

Sacred icons have long been considered in the West as *windows to heaven, theology in color,* or as some Early Church council fathers put it (paraphrased) *the Gospel for the spiritually illiterate* – portals to the threshold of the supernatural many do not know about, while others desire to see, but have not yet seen. Unlike religious paintings, icons are neither the sum of their above parts, nor just the simplistic definitions given; or even the distorted, unsmiling and at times disproportionately elongated representations of human persons now living in the fullness of the Divine Light.

Icons are neither one of the seven sacraments of the universal Church, nor mere sacramentals as often understood in the Western Church. They are a cross between the former and the latter. This because:

1. the grace with which they become invested, after having been named and officially blessed in church, results in icons often becoming wonder-working in unabashed ways that some consider to be unbelievably outrageous, if not downright unbelievable;

2. any relative worship offered to icons by people passes on directly to whoever is depicted therein – namely *the honor which is shown them is referred to the prototypes which those images represent* (Council of Trent); and

3. the portrayed representations in icons are *not like the original with respect to essence, but with respect to hypostasis* (Nicaea II). This includes the divine hypostases.

The worship referred to above is that of *proskynesis* (i.e., veneration), not *latreia* (i.e., adoration and absolute worship), which latter is reserved for God alone.

Icons, moreover, differ from religious paintings in the following ways:

1. They are not just portraits of people, but *prototypes of the future human person-within-the-Church* (Saint Evgenii Nikolaevich Trubetskoi) – namely, the deified person, in keeping with the bold and oft-repeated proclamation of Jesus Christ: *I said, you are gods* (Jn 10:34);

2. The *light of the first day and of the eighth day meet in the icon [because it is] always characterized by the unity of creation, Christology and eschatology* (Paul Evdokimov). Thus, icons and frescos written in traditional iconographic style possess both a liturgical function and a theophanic ministry, uniting the meaning and presence of God in the light of the Transfiguration on Mount Tabor;

3. By their carefully planned, internal geometric structure, as well as their design and deliberate restraint, icons facilitate a sense of stillness, order, quietude and peace – a sense of spiritual transcendence - in both people and the environment in which they are found. These

factors are commonly absent from, or actively worked against by, the sentimentalized and/or sensualized representations of God, the saints and the angels found in much of the religious art of the West. The latter, in fact, facilitates the natural, rather than the supernatural, by exciting the flesh instead of the spirit;

4. By virtue of #2 and #3 as these interact with grace, icons can facilitate the opening up of the heart of people's souls, counteracting that *darkness and blindness of the spirit [which is] a symptom of the crisis of man's very existence* (Benedict XVI);

5. Through #2 and #3, icons can effectively convey the beauty and presence of God during the apophatic darkness (more commonly known in the West as the dark night of the soul), not just during the cataphatic presentation of the Christian life;

6. Icons are embodied prayer, created in prayer and for prayer by the driving force that is *the love of God and yearning for Him as perfect beauty* (Archimandrite Zenon);

7. Icons are *the fruit of contemplation, [coming] from an interior vision and thus lead[ing] us to such an interior vision . . . in communion with the seeing faith of the*

Church, [with] the ecclesial dimension [being] essential (Benedict XVI); and

8. They speak *about dogmatic truths revealed to human beings in Scripture and Tradition, [being] anthropological in content, while reflecting the eschatological, redeemed and deified state of nature, [with a] liturgical and mystical purpose* (Metropolitan Alfeyev).

Thus, why are icons so needed in the Church today?

THE NEW ICONOCLASM

Iconoclasm constitutes heresy (Nicaea II).

Go into a Catholic church in the West – in particular, a new or recently-built church – and you can be forgiven for thinking that you have, all of a sudden, entered into either a spaceship reminiscent of *Star Trek* or the auditorium of a theater, or even just a garage, despite all the money spent, time consumed and planners planned. Wreckovators, under the name of liturgists or liturgical consultants, have elevated the natural – or worse – over the supernatural, oftentimes without knowing the underlying spiritual consequences of their wreckovations as long as the creations resultant from their ideas were, in effect if not in intent, made in their own image under the rationalization of being 'hip' and 'with the times.'

All that might be well and good as far as reason goes. After all, we are in the 21ˢᵗ century and reason has, for the most part, become decontextualized from faith and reified in its own right. But how is any of that going to quieten the flesh and still the soul, while engaging all your senses, to help you pray and give you a tangible experience of the timelessness, infinite presence and similarly infinite love of God?

Icons and the sacred art of iconography, considered in the context of the universal Church, have grown directly out of the grass-roots struggle of the People of God *with the kingdom and the image of the beast* (Trubetskoi) – namely, that kingdom reported in Scripture whereby *All these things will I give you, if you fall down and worship me* (Mt 4:7). As embodied prayer that facilitates more prayer, the opening of one's heart and the possible re-opening of the heart of one's soul through grace, resulting as a consequence in the elevation of one's spirit to God, icons can fill souls with a vision of a very different truth about life, existential meaning and the world. Icons provide the determinants of a truth that, of necessity and by attraction, draws people into the otherworldly vision of the City of God (Augustine of Hippo). The quiet drama portrayed in icons facilitates the reassurance that *the destruction left by the beast and his kingdom are not all in all, but there is another meaning to life and it shall prevail* (Trubetskoi). And this occurs despite the present, conscious veneration of the image of the beast, part of which is the new iconoclasm in the Church, especially that taking place in the Catholic Church.

Icons, with their created beauty that is both a mediated and an endowed tiny presentation of the Uncreated Beauty Who Is God, have the power of providing spiritual strength to people. Through said beauty, they are also capable of making people hunger or develop a hunger for the inheritance that is the birthright of each individual, in particular the Christian – namely, that infinite and eternal place of Divine Light, which is both God and the Father's House.

Are icons needed in the Church today?

You decide.

Some Responses, Questions and Elaborations

Audience member: It is extraordinarily hard for a Western mind to wrap itself around the concept of an icon, even if that mind has an affinity towards Christian Neo-Platonism, which gets close to being able to philosophically articulate that which an icon is to the West. The West tends to have statues rather than icons.

Statues, though, are not icons as statues invoke their subject, but icons have a true participation in their subject so that where an icon is, there exists a certain presence of the subject, someplace between a sacrament and sacramental presence. It is not a 'real' presence as Christ is really present in the Eucharist. It less of a presence than Christ's sacramental presence in the liturgical action of Baptism, yet more than Christ's sacramental presence in the reading of Scripture . . . An icon [gives] a certain manifestation of the presence of that person, a prayer in oil and pigment that neither indicates nor invokes, but makes present the presence of the individual through which the physical reality of the icon places us into contact with.

The West recoils at the thought of the saints, let alone God, having a presence here and now with it. Protestantism is much more comfortable with God being over there, not here and now. The classical themes of iconoclasm, of the pagan, heretical Catholic or Protestant varieties boil down to the revulsion in man for a God who walks with us and who brings along with Him in His courtiers, who are approved not by man, but by God. The West is okay with a God that is close, but not too close. The icon makes God too close and that is why iconoclasm must be a hallmark of the modern religious experience.

Author: Exactly! Icons and their method of 'being' go directly against the Western worldview and the very fact of their true participation – not just symbolic remembrance of the portrayed subject – is something not many successfully wrap their minds around.

I have given up counting the number of times I have heard the question: "But isn't an icon the same as a painting or a statue?"

And this question arises even from people who are supposed to know better within the institutional Church itself. Further, the locatedness of icons between true sacraments and sacramentals often leaves people thinking either a mistake is being made, or the persons elaborating the topic are ignorant, heretic or both. None of which is the case.

In the East, the "certain presence of the subject," as you say, which leads to the icon-as-participation rather than icon-as-symbolic-remembrance, is considered to arise from the icon having been invested with the *energeia* of God when named and blessed. It should be noted that this is neither the essence of God, which can be considered tantamount to His nature, nor just His grace. Both naming and blessing of the icon are also necessary, not just the former or the latter. In the West, however, the best we seem to have come up with so far in relation to terminology has been *grace* as a word to define things, so many subtleties in terms of *how* an icon is invested with grace and *what* kind of grace this is, compared to that in paintings and statues, has remained absent from both the theological and popular discourses. Thus, a *de facto* contribution has been both made and maintained in the Western Church to foreclosing the provision of an appropriate understanding of icons and how they operate in relation to God.

Now, a few things need to be clarified:

1. You said that an icon is "a prayer in oil and pigment." Since time immemorial, icons have been written primarily using water, not oil. This because it was more easily accessible, cheaper and part of the providence of God right from the beginning of the creation narrative in the Book of Genesis. The very process of writing an icon, including how the gold or silver leaf, or both, is applied and how the levels of the icon are built up, is considered to theologically mirror the process that was employed by God when He created the universe. The iconographer is thus considered to become a co-creator with God to make the icon participatory. Using oil, or even synthetics, for icons is a relatively late invention – if it can even be called that. Moreover, if you are in the company of a purist, you will hear the

rebuttal that icons written in oil directly violate tradition. In other words, oil is a short-cut of the writing process. That being said, oil is certainly easier to use than water;

2. You said that an icon "neither indicates nor invokes." I disagree. Specifically, when one prays in front of an icon, one is directly invoking the participatory presence that is in the icon, with such an invocation then being directly transferred to the holy or divine person/s portrayed therein;

3. You added that "Protestantism is much more comfortable with God being over there, not here and now." I respond that even Catholicism is doing this to some degree, albeit to a lesser extent. It is not just a "revulsion in man for a God who walks with us" that we are seeing, but an actual revulsion against God Who wants to be in us, not just with us. Such a phenomenon is happening within Catholicism itself;

4. You said that "The West is okay with a God that is close, but not too close." That point is precisely why we need icons even more in the West today, because the Father Himself wants to be (and has always wanted to be, since day one) with us in a way that is "too close," rather than just close.

Audience member: Would you mind sharing your thoughts on reproductions of icons – the laminated cardstock/varnished onto wood variety?

I would say that an icon conveys the presence even in the absence of the viewer invoking anything at all. An icon of the Theotokos is still a certain manifestation of the Virgin's presence even if the parish is empty.

It might be argued that what worth there is in modern Western mysticism is the exploration of man himself as a living icon of God. What is modern Western society but self-hatred of itself, of man being an icon of God? Western society hates icons and hates itself all the more because it has glimpsed in its mystics, man as icon. Thus, everything that gave rise to this thought must be destroyed, including the icon itself.

Author: *Energeia* does not equate with the term *grace,* as we know. Yet some people remain unable to comprehend the difference. *Energeia* is precisely what icons are invested with upon being named and blessed. It is what differentiates them from religious paintings and statues. Here is an easy exercise to make this concept more easily understood: Place an icon that has been named and blessed next to a religious painting. Let a couple of days go by, then stand or sit in front of them. In front of which one do you feel more at peace? The icon or the painting?

I detest icon reproductions – the "laminated/cardstock variety" – with a passion. Not only do such 'reproductions' circumvent the writing process that a prayer in itself, a labor of love to Love. There is also a 'feel' to them, which makes it very clear that they are unlike the originals. Carry out the above exercise with this kind of reproduction substituted for the religious painting and you will see the difference. That being said, icon reproductions can be wonder-working, should God choose to do so – reports of oil or myrrh streaming from them are numerous, throughout the centuries right up to this day. Such reproductions are naturally much cheaper, more affordable, than original icons as they are mass-produced. And then there arises the question of execution – namely, has the icon been poorly or masterfully reproduced? Several levels exist.

As regards the phenomenon of invoking, you are correct. The icon does invoke the participatory presence when prayer is said. That said, regardless of whether one is praying in front of the icon or not, the presence remains. Once again, this is part of the difference between icons and paintings or statues.

About the question of Christianity and the God Who desires intimacy, I agree. Many Catholics "are more comfortable with a God that is not too close." Yet, that is not Catholicism itself. It is what Catholicism has tended to become these days in the West. Many, many people are scared of God, in particular of the Father. But all God has ever wanted – and still wants – from each one of us can be boiled down to two things: intimacy and love. It is that simple. If you really love someone with your whole heart, soul, mind and being (Mt 22:37), why would you not want to be close? Protestantism is "predicated on desiring a God to be close but not too close" because it was based on rebellion, not love.

Regarding the issue of iconoclasm, what we are witnessing now in the Western Church is fast reaching the point of superceding the previous iconoclastic periods. This time, however, two major differences exist: (A) the iconoclasm is not coming from without, but from within the Church itself. It is not imposed by an external authority; and (B) there is no grass-roots opposition or resistance to it from the people. The latter is the reason why it has been so successful thus far. In previous iconoclastic periods, there was internal destruction in the Church, yes; but the people strongly resisted to the point of creating even more icons, learning more about them, training more people 'underground,' hiding the icons in their homes, venerating them, and so on and so forth. This latter factor is now missing as a whole. That is why the destruction we are witnessing keeps spreading in the way it already has.

About the subject of man as an icon of God, it is this! This is exactly where the inversion is still occurring. You cannot have man as true icon of God unless man remains linked to God in his heart and soul in the first place. Otherwise, where is Life? You end up with man as an icon of something else – or someone else. This process is at the very heart of what we are seeing and why it is iconoclastic. We have ended up with the image of the beast being perpetuated (unknowingly by most) rather than the image of God, which has become largely covered up. But this does not mean that the situation must remain so.

WHAT IS TRUTH? ICONS REVEALED

There exists the icon of the Holy Trinity by Saint Andrei Rublev; therefore, God exists (Saint Pavel Florenski).

In our 21st century Western world, base and over-saturated with materiality and sensuality – a growing wasteland that, for the most part, neither knows nor does it want to know God – icons are silent, but active, witnesses to the truth. They are an ever-present act of *being* and defiance in the face of those who would eradicate or cover up the very Face of God from His earth. Icons sing the songs of angels as they remain hung on walls, stuck on shelves or hidden in storage closets, and do not speak. They praise the Lord of hosts despite being unable to move. They testify without cease to the Divine Life even as they possess no life of their own. But as Pontius Pilate said: *What is truth?* (Jn 18:38).

In the Last Supper discourse, Christ proclaimed: *I am the Way, the Truth and the Life. No one comes to the Father except through Me* (Jn 14:6). It is also common knowledge that icons have their theological basis in the Incarnation. In what other ways do icons witness to the Truth?

God Is Beauty and Beautiful

Beauty will save the world (Fyodor Mikhailovich Dostoevski).

The British poet John Keats said: *Beauty is truth and truth is beauty.* But the sixth century theologian Dionysus the Aeropagite had already declared that God is beautiful and Beauty, with the latter in actuality being one of the divine names. Saint Thomas Aquinas and Saint Augustine concurred in their *Summa Theologica* and *Confessions* respectively. The fourth century monk Evagrius Ponticus declared that the spirit of beauty was the Holy Spirit, whereas the theologian Paul Evdokimov clarified that it is the Spirit Who, in reality, is the divine iconographer when icons are being written in

20

an appropriate manner. Saint Joseph of Volokolamsk added that *It is not the object (the physical icon) which is venerated, but the Beauty which, by resemblance, the icon transmits mysteriously.*

The Father is greater than I (Jn 14:28).

Jesus Christ, the only-begotten Son of God, is the Truth by His own proclamation. But He is also Beauty not just due to His divine nature, Kingship and glory, but because He is the *Vera Icona* of the Father – Ineffable Beauty Himself and the Fount of all beauty – as revealed to the human person by Him who is the Spirit of beauty. It was Christ the Icon who gave us the first icon through the cloth He sent to King Abgar of Edessa by one of the 70 disciples (cf. Lk 10:1), Thaddeus of Edessa, to heal Abgar of his illness at the personal invitation of the latter. This rectangular piece of cloth, upon placed in the hands of Abgar together with a short letter bearing Christ's dictated reply to him, was found to bear the image of the Savior imprinted upon it (*Codex Vossianus Latinus Q 69*). The Mandylion of Edessa is thus the first material icon to be given by God to humanity. The beautiful Father had sent His Icon to earth both to feed a starving world with the Bread of Life, through the institution of the Holy Eucharist, and to lift its darkened spirits with a bit of His divine beauty through the institution of holy icons, all of which manifest the Divine Light.

Icons, therefore, insofar as they are beautifully-made and bring forth all the exquisiteness possible within their power through a certain level of skill, in combination with prayer and the action of the Holy Spirit, witness with volumes of concurrent eloquence and silence to the Beauty Who is Truth from even before their investiture with the *energeia* of God upon being named and blessed. According to Leonid Ouspensky, they stand *on a level with the Holy Scriptures and with the Cross, as one of the forms of revelation and knowledge of God, in which Divine and human will and action become blended.* Icons present aesthetic beauty to the sensory eye of the beholder and transcendent beauty to his or her spiritual eye, thus capturing and facilitating the elevation of the person's spirit to God.

The Ugliness of the Beast

Non possumus amare nisi pulchra (Saint Augustine).
Ugliness.   Hideousness.   Facelessness. Meaninglessness. Desolateness.
The void.
Taken   together,   iconoclasm.   A   polite ecclesiastical euphemism for totalitarianism.
All of them are no more and no less than the marks – the 'footprints' – of the beast and of his abyss

(cf. Rv 13:16-18). All of the above, in essence and in fact, are more expansive and multi-varied facets of that specific phenomenon known as the abomination of desolation that had been spoken about by the prophet Daniel (cf. Dn 9:27; Mt 24:15). All of them have one, single aim: to eradicate from the face of both the Church and the earth not just the likeness of God, which is already fractured to differing degrees in human persons, but the very image of God from the face of all humanity.

The beast knows that neither himself, nor his cronies and their agents – the latter, willing or unwilling – can ever eradicate the *invisible* image of God that is imprinted upon the heart of the soul of the human person. That is there to stay. It is untouchable, no matter whether the heart of that soul is open or closed. However, the beast also knows that if he can succeed in covering up that image with layer upon layer, upon layer on yet another layer of grime, ugliness, hideousness, facelessness, meaninglessness, desolateness and sin, he will have won a large part of the battle in making his own the heart and mind of that person. And the preceding step to achieving that victory in an easier way on a mass scale is precisely to eradicate the *visible* image of God from the face of both the Church and the earth.

Without beauty, there is nothing left in the world worth doing (Paul Evdokimov).

The image – namely, the holy icon – is not just *a* part of Christianity. It is an *intrinsic* part of Christianity itself, instituted by Christ Himself. Get rid of the icon, which as we have seen is an icon of the Icon of the Father and this *regardless of the deified person who is depicted therein*, and you will have succeeded in eliminating a major obstacle to getting rid of Christianity itself. This take place by wiping out the visible image of God from the hearts and minds of humankind.

The icon provides wounded and struggling humanity, believers and non-believers alike, with the healing power of both the beauty of God and God who is Beauty Himself. As declared by Christ in the Sermon on the Mount: *Your heavenly Father makes his sun rise on the bad and the good* (Mt 5:45). The icon thus splits apart the rule of the beast and saves humanity from eternal destruction. Get rid of beauty by getting rid of the icon and the Real Presence of Christ in the Eucharist, and you will have gotten rid of God.

ICONS AS RESISTANCE

In times past albeit not remote, icons were a strong part of the resistance in the Church against the iconoclasm and oppression *du jour*. They can still be used very effectively in this way.

The people would buy one icon or more from either a master-iconographer or the advanced students in the master's workshop. They would then have it blessed and set it up with ceremony in their home. People unable to afford an original icon would make sacrifices to buy one; that is how vital the icon was considered to be in regard to one's relationship with God, one's faith and the Christian spiritual journey. They would never dream of buying something plastic when this started to exist. Others would trade some of the tools they used in everyday life – for example, farmer's tools – for a real icon until they could pay for it. Yet others would take lessons over a period of time in order to learn how to write an icon or two for themselves, which was cheaper in the long run than buying a single icon outright – in particular, if one then managed to get set up writing icons for the whole neighborhood. These kinds of icons are known as *popular* icons due to their lack of sufficient finesse in comparison to those written by the masters. They tended to be very prevalent in Ukraine.

Other people would learn to write icons by studying several older icons in depth, with the icons *per se* being the real teachers. Many Russian master-iconographers started out that way because they were often so poor, they could not afford to take lessons. Some others, including priests and the laity, would defend the icon against usurpers and potential usurpers with their own lives. In return, God would reward the people for their faith with nothing less than spectacular shows of His divine intervention. These shows often paralleled those of the Old Testament era with regard to their largesse and their physical impossibility by natural means. But the fact remains that God still acts in such a manner, to this day, where icons are concerned.

Icons Hidden, but Triumphant

You deigned to reveal Your face to me like a formless sun (Symeon the New Theologian).

According to Saint Pavel Florenski, icons should be the product of revelation, not mass production. Benedict XVI said the same thing. Some original icons have relics embedded in them. Others do not. Some are covered in part with precious stones and/or *riza* - a 'robe' or covering made of precious metals. Some are enshrined in a *kiot* — a beautifully hand-carved wooden frame that, not infrequently, costs as much as the icon itself, if not more, due to its intricate work. Other icons are placed on a shelf in a prayer corner or hung on the wall. Some icons are adorned with a *rushnyk* — a hand-woven, colored towel that has a distinctive pattern and is used to handle the icon so as not to dirty it with oil from one's fingerprints. Other icons are adorned with flowers. All icons, however, are the focus of veneration, fostering and facilitating prayer of the heart. They are made to be kissed with love, the kisses given being transferred to the prototype.

In the home, the original icon is placed in the main room where the family gathers and which preferably faces east. This icon takes the place of what has become known these days as 'your television.' According to Saint Nicodemus the Hagiorite, pure beeswax candle made from the combs of hives should be kept lit in front of the icon for the following reasons:

1. To glorify God Who is both Light and Who has brought forth the Light of the world;
2. As an offering to the depicted prototype;
3. To denote that the light of Christ has dispelled all the darkness;
4. To honor the martyrs for the Faith;
5. To manifest the inner joy that may be present in our souls;
6. To symbolize any good works we may have done; and
7. As a reminder that if we turn to God, our sins and the sins of those for whom we pray shall be forgiven and burned away.

All the colors in an icon have meaning; none of them are arbitrary. Here are some meanings of the most frequent colors that can be found in an original icon (Irina Yazykova):

1. Red is the color of the earth, blood, sacrifice and royalty;
2. Blue denotes the divinity, the heavens, purity and having been chosen;
3. Green is the color of the Holy Spirit, eternal life and blossoming in God;
4. White denotes the transfiguration, purity and the robes of those who do justice;
5. Purple denotes royalty; whereas
6. Black is the color of darkness, the grave and the abyss.

Darker shades of the above tend to indicate the impeccable brilliance of the Divine Light that has often been perceived by humanity as blinding darkness (i.e., the apophatic darkness). The gold or silver halo around the head of the depicted prototype also denotes the Light and indicates that the person is a saint, angel or divine Person. Any persons portrayed without halos have either not yet become saints or pertain to evil.

A Brief Theology of Pure Beeswax Candles

Blessed are the pure in heart for they shall see God (Mt 5:8).

One hundred percent pure beeswax candles are used, to be lit in front of the icon – not 51% 'pure' as per the latest USCCB guidelines, or something made out of paraffin that you buy at the *Dollar Store*. The main reasons for this are as follows, with some reasons coming from Saint Symeon of Thessaloniki:

1. God the Father is the Provider. Everything that is offered to Him in an original icon written in accordance with traditional practice comes from the earth and its animals. No man-made materials are used. Even the brushes employed for painting the icon come from the tails of animals. The offering returned to God, therefore, when the icon is installed, comes from His own provision to humanity. That is why only natural, primary materials should be employed. In a parallel manner, the candles used to light up the icon should come directly from the bees He created, not from secondary materials. Using candles of pure beeswax indicates one's faith that the Father will, indeed, provide during times of hardship for His people, the family or the person concerned,

as He had done for the Israelites after their exodus from Egypt;

2. The purity of the beeswax symbolizes the purity that should be in our hearts and souls. God is pure; He is Immaculate. As such, He cannot live where the darkness of sin resides, even though He has never stopped desiring to come and live not just *with* us, but *in* us – namely, in the very heart of our souls as He had lived in Adam and Eve during the first days of creation, and as He has lived in a handful of human persons who have resided fully in the Divine Will;

3. Beeswax candles give off a sweet and delicate scent. This scent is considered to symbolize the sweet aroma that should emanate from our souls as a result of divine grace;

4. Candles made out of pure beeswax are supple, regardless of whether they are thick or thin. This quality symbolizes the flexibility that should characterize our hearts and souls until they have been made firm by the Gospel; and

5. As the pure candles feed the flame while they burn, they symbolize our struggle on the Christian journey with the necessary, but beautiful, processes of purification, illumination and deification.

DISCERNING ICONS GOOD AND BAD

The purpose of an icon is to take us into the realm of the Spirit, where we can experience the transforming power of divine grace (John Baggley).

Audience member: From where can one find icons to acquire, if one wishes to get a few for the home? Which are good icons to get? From which icons should one stay miles away?

Author: The above is a hot topic in this day and age of non-discrimination. It holds most true if one does not have thousands of dollars to shell out to acquire various icons written by known and reputable masters – or to settle a lawsuit alleging discrimination by having dared to prefer in public, in writing, some iconographers over others, without sufficient and documented 'empirical evidence.' But since it has always been my fortune – or misfortune? – to not be tongue-tied regardless of the hat worn at whatever point in time, I will answer these questions as best I can.

A Brief Guide to Choosing an Icon

The beautiful and the good, ultimately the beautiful and God, coincide. Through the appearance of the beautiful, we are wounded in our innermost being, and that wound grips us and takes us beyond ourselves; it stirs longing into flight and moves us toward the truly Beautiful to the Good in itself (Benedict XVI).

First, when considering an acquisition, bear in mind that an icon is not just made for prayer, but has been made *because* of prayer. This is a vital factor in any choices to be made. Would you thus get an icon branded *Made in China/Vietnam/Taiwan/wherever?* Or would you get an icon written by an independent iconographer, master or not-yet-master, who tries to follow the life of the Faith?

Ask around for the latter. You might be pleasantly surprised by the terms some lesser-known iconographers might give you, in particular if they are creating icons for love of God (as they should be), rather than just being out to make money no matter what. Do not be shy to use that time-honored tradition known in more popular parlance as *haggling*. Iconographers being craftspeople for the most part in the old school mindset understand it very well. That having been said, bear in mind that holy icons of the portable variety take about 45 hours to write and that does not include the time spent waiting for them to dry and varnishing them with *olifa* when ready. Larger icons obviously take longer.

Second, do not restrict yourself to your locality, region or nation, when looking for an affordable icon. Prices differ hugely between independent iconographers in the West and their counterparts in Eastern Europe or

Russia. For example, I have managed to get icons from the latter group of iconographers for about one-fifth of the price often quoted by iconographers in the United States. But how can one find these kinds of icons – icons that *should* have been (and have been) written, rather than just *produced* – without having a trained eye or just plain, good old-fashioned knowing people?

Third, look at the face. I cannot stress this enough. *Look at the face.* The face and its expression in an icon are a dead giveaway as to whether that icon has been written or not as a result of prayer. What does that face do for you? What do you experience when you look at that face, that expression? Do you feel stricken in your soul? *Wounded by love,* as Benedict XVI said? Or do you feel repulsed? Do you feel peace, calmness, quietude – joy, even – when looking at that icon? Or do you feel fear or that 'something's not quite right?' *This* is the key to discerning proper icons from those arising as a product of diabolical influences. The latter do exist.

An icon is a handwritten image that is often the result of direct or indirect revelation to the heart of the soul of the iconographer before and during the writing process itself. That image bears upon it the 'imprint' of the Icon of God through the divine *energeia* as discussed earlier. But so does your soul if you are in a state of grace! The icon and your soul thus should be 'speaking' to each other in an analogous, albeit not similar, manner to when Christ 'spoke' to John *in utero* and John recognized Him through the Holy Spirit, when Mary and Elizabeth met while both of them were pregnant (Lk 1:41). If the icon does not somehow 'speak' to you when gazing upon it, the question arises: What is missing in that icon? Is it just an apparent lack of technical skill – something that can be easily attained with further practice – or is it something else altogether?

On the one hand, if the iconographer is pursuing holiness, that pursuit is going to be seen and felt, one way or another, in the icon regardless of skill level. This because one of the effects of genuine iconography on the painter is the opening up wide of one's heart and, at times, even the very heart of the soul by the grace of God. That is, therefore, going to come through even in icons written in the crudest way. The aforementioned process occurs because it is the Holy Spirit who is in reality the divine iconographer and genuine icons (for lack of better terminology) are intimately related to the various stages and processes of theosis and deification.

On the other hand, if an iconographer is painting an icon under the influence of false light, there is going to be a closing, not opening, of the heart and that closure is going to be transmitted to the final product. This becomes most evident in the depicted face and its expression, since it is precisely there that defacement — the destruction or eradication of the image, *iconoclasm* of the imprint within an icon itself — first occurs and with the greatest intensity possible. In other words, what is present in the depths of the heart and soul of the iconographer is going to come out without fail in the icon and if you are in a state of grace when gazing upon it, you should be able to easily discern its underlying origin. This process occurs irrespective of the amount of control or otherwise exerted by the iconographer in relation to the final product.

Fourth, given all of the above, you can reach some conclusions as to what or what not to acquire and from where, when it comes to sacred icons. If you see an icon of the "cardstock variety" that is beautiful and it really 'speaks' to you, and you also see a handwritten icon that you feel pushes you away, it is the former that you should acquire despite its materiality, not the latter. That for reasons now obvious.

Enjoy your journey with icons.

About the Author

Marcelle Bartolo-Abela is a Maltese-American consultant on the interface of multiculturalism, psychology, spirituality, and the political sphere. A first-generation immigrant to America, she served as a mental health clinician in hospital, community, private practice settings in the Northeast US and Malta. She has lectured on psychology and psychotherapy to psychiatry residents and graduate students in the US, UK, and Malta. She served as consultant to faculty and program managers on the combined provision of multicultural psychology and spirituality services. She also provided advocacy and consultation on free speech rights in relation to criminalization discourses in the legislative agenda *First Malta Then the World.* Bartolo-Abela is the author of nine books on the Catholic Faith including *Deification of Man in Christianity, The Icon of the Divine Heart of God the Father: Apologia and Canon,* and *Who Are You? What is Your Faith? America's 21ˢᵗ Century Alt-Right and Catholic Social Doctrine.* She holds a Master of Science in Psychology from Springfield College, the Postgraduate Certificate in Research Methodologies in the Social Sciences from Middlesex University, and the Certificate in Catholic Social Doctrine for Professionals from The Catholic University of America. Bartolo-Abela is a mid-level apprentice in Russian-Byzantine iconography. Her icons can be found in churches and private collections in the US, Italy, and Malta.

www.ingramcontent.com/pod-product-compliance
Lightning Source LLC
Chambersburg PA
CBHW071015120726
47910CB00004B/1525